The Happy Heart

written and illustrated by Matthew Keown

For Reilly

The Happy Heart goes "Lub-dub" all day.
"Lub-dub! Lub-dub!" The Happy Heart asks
its friends to play.

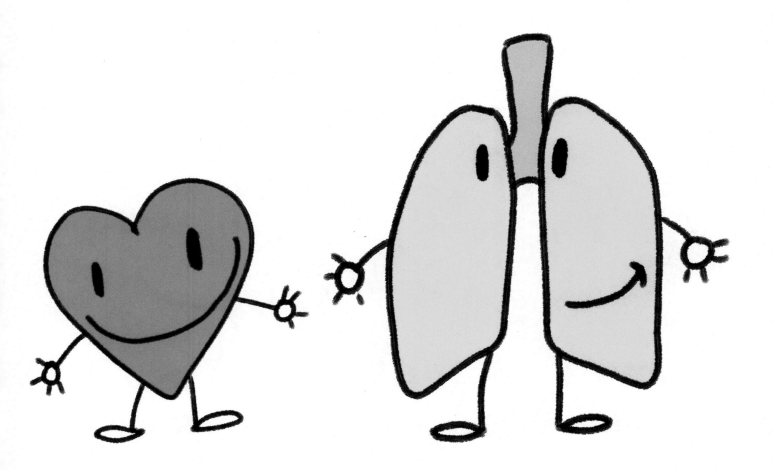

The Happy Heart visits the lungs.
"Do you want to play, Mr. Lungs?" asks Happy.
"I'm sorry, Happy, I need to breathe in air all
day. I don't have time to play," the lungs reply.

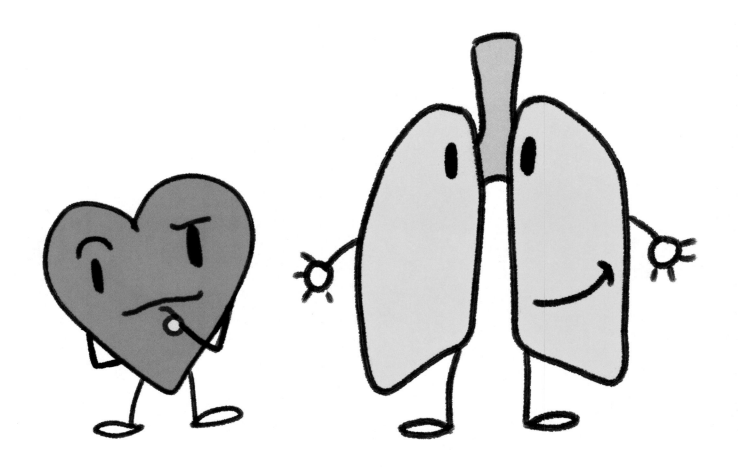

"Can I breathe the air too?" Happy asks.
"You're a heart, Happy," says the lungs.
"You can't breathe the air. You'll have
to find somewhere else to go."

The Happy Heart visits the liver.
"Do you have time to play, Miss Liver?" asks Happy.
"No, Happy, I have to clean the body," replies
the liver, "I don't have any time to play."

"Can I clean the body too?" Happy asks.
"I'm sorry, Happy, you're a heart," says the liver.
"You can't clean the body. Run along now and
find a new friend."

Happy visits the stomach.
"Do you want to play, Mrs. Stomach?" Happy asks.
"I'm too busy today, Happy," says the stomach.
"I have to digest all this food! I don't have time
to play with you."

"Can I help digest the food?" Happy asks.
"You're a heart, Happy!" replies the stomach.
"You can't digest food. You'll have to find
something else to do."

Happy visits the intestines.
"Want to play, Mr. Intestines?" Happy asks.
"I'm sorry, Happy, I'm too busy absorbing the nutrients from food. I have no time to play."

"Can I absorb the nutrients?" Happy asks.
"I don't think so, Happy," replies the intestines,
"you're a heart, you can't absorb any nutrients.
You'll have to find someone else to play with."

This made the Happy Heart sad.

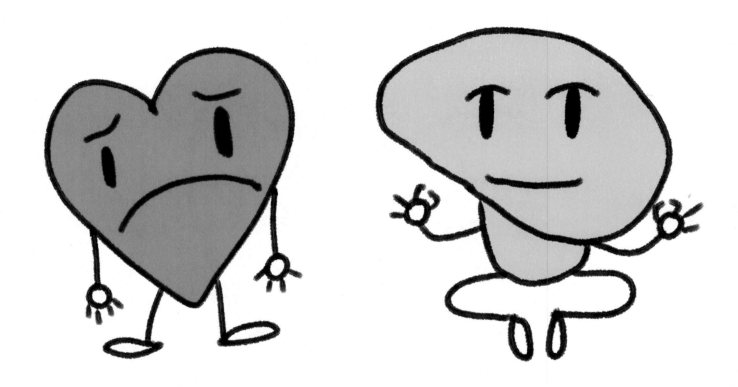

The Happy Heart visits the wise brain.
"Mr. Brain, I'm sad. Everyone is busy and
I can't do all the things that they do.
I feel like I'm useless."

"Don't say that, Happy," the brain says.
"You're the most important one of all!"
"I am?" Happy asks.

"You lub-dub all day! without your lub-dubs we couldn't do what we do," the brain explains. "Because you lub-dub, the stomach can digest; the lungs can breathe; the liver can clean and the intestines can absorb nutrients."

"Without your lub-dub, I can't think and tell everyone to do their jobs. You make all of us possible."
The Happy Heart became excited.
"Really, Mr. Brain?"

The wise brain explains to the Happy Heart
that he does even more than that.
The Happy Heart makes us feel love.
The Happy Heart makes us work hard
when things get tough.
The Happy Heart warms us when we
feel our parents' touch.

This made the Happy Heart happy again!

The Happy Heart thanked the wise brain.
The wise brain made the Happy Heart
realize how important it was.

So the Happy Heart went "Lub-dub! Lub-dub!"
all the rest of the day.

The End.

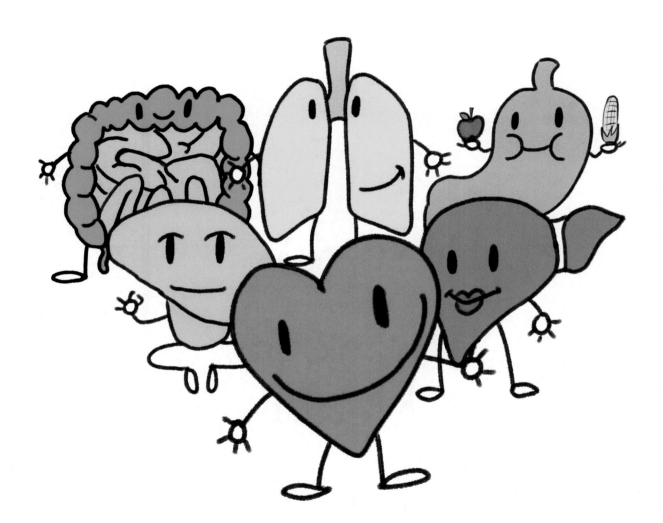

Thank you
for reading.